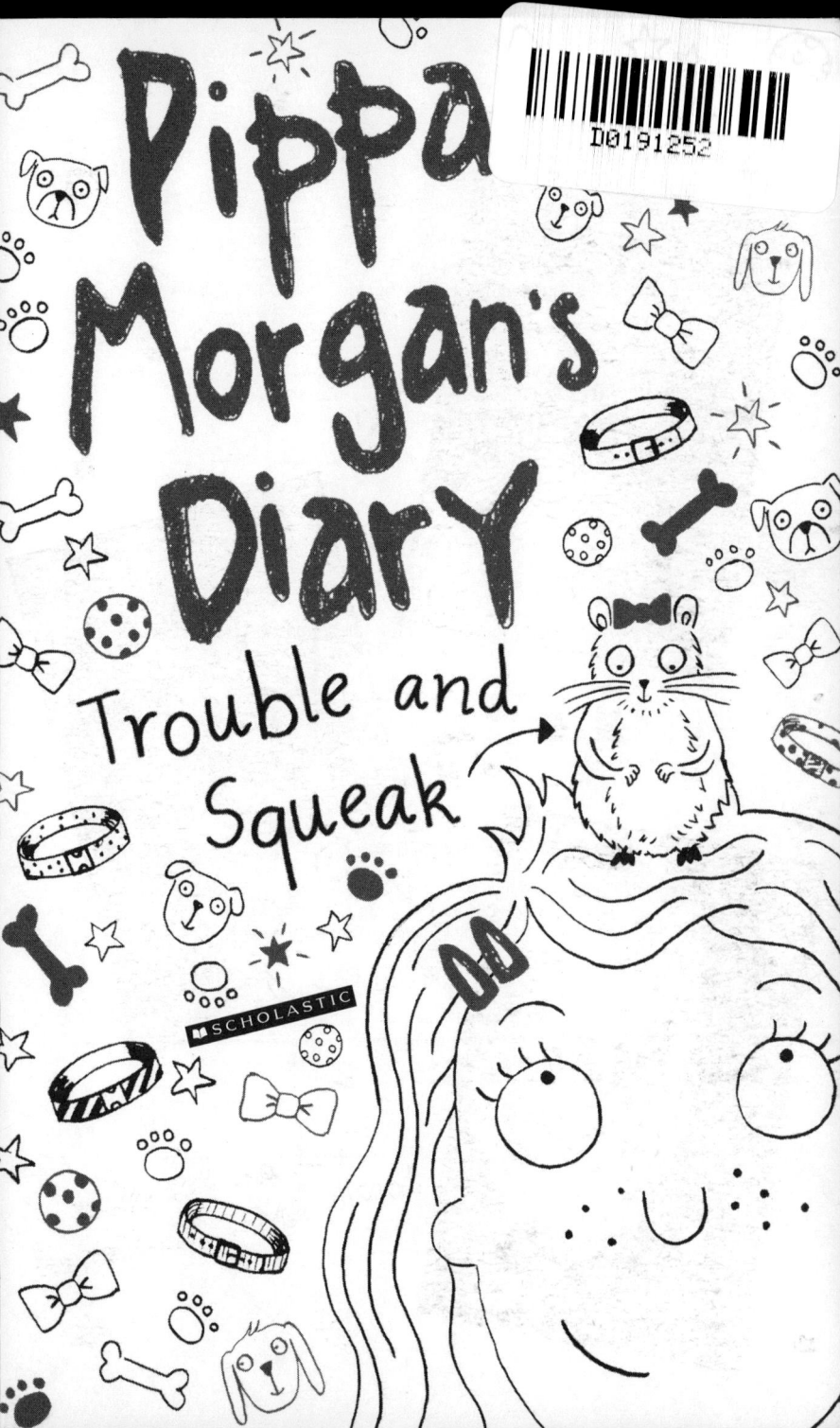

Pippa Morgan's Diary

Trouble and Squeak

SCHOLASTIC

First published in the UK in 2016 by Scholastic Children's Books
An imprint of Scholastic Ltd
Euston House, 24 Eversholt Street
London, NW1 1DB, UK
Registered office: Westfield Road, Southam, Warwickshire, CV47 0RA
SCHOLASTIC and associated logos are trademarks and/
or registered trademarks of Scholastic Inc.

Text copyright © Hothouse Fiction Limited, 2016
Illustration copyright © Kate Larsen, 2016

The rights of Annie Kelsey and Kate Larsen to be identified as the
author and illustrator of this work have been asserted by them.

ISBN 978 1407 16230 0

A CIP catalogue record for this book is available from the British Library.

Printed and bound by CPI Group (UK) Ltd, Croydon, CR0 4YY
Papers used by Scholastic Children's Books
are made from wood grown in sustainable forests.

1 3 5 7 9 10 8 6 4 2

www.scholastic.co.uk

Squeaks of thanks
to Kate Cary!

<u>Wednesday evening –</u>
<u>on the sofa</u>

I'm so glad I have my diary! Mum has
banned me from saying "puppy" for the
rest of the day. She says I've talked
about nothing else for weeks and her
ears need a rest. (I didn't know ears
could get tired.) But she says I can write
about puppies as much as I like. So I'm
curled up on the sofa with my diary and
my favourite pen (which has puppies on it.
OF COURSE!).

There are SO many reasons I should have
a puppy. When I think about them all, my

head fizzes. I wonder if it will pop off like a champagne cork?

I'd better make a list so that I don't have to think about them all at the same time. Then my head won't pop off.

<u>Reasons I Should Have a Puppy</u>

I would be happy FOR EVER (Dog People are happier than Non-Dog People. I did an online quiz, so I know).

The puppy would be happy FOR EVER because I am going to be the best dog owner in the world.

🐶 A dog would keep Mum company when I stay at Dad's. Mum says she doesn't need company, even though Dad moved out ages ago. But I don't believe her. I'd hate to be in the house on my own.

🐶 I would get really fit taking it for walks.

🐶 I would never be bored again, EVER.

🐶 A dog would keep us safe from burglars. The king of China used to keep a Pekingese up his sleeve to protect him from assassins.

(I wish my sleeves were big enough to keep dogs in.) And a dog is the best fire alarm in the world.

I could train it to find things, which would be great because Mum is always losing her keys/purse/phone/TV remote.

It could eat all our leftovers (no more Fridge Surprise Suppers! Hurray!).

If me or Mum ever go blind, it could be our guide dog.

Just, squeeeee!!!!!!!!!

I've just read my list and I can't believe
I don't already have a puppy! There are
SO MANY reasons! I think I will stick my
list on the fridge so Mum can see it too.
Then she'd understand how important it
is we get a puppy straight away. I've asked
her a gazillion times but she says that it
would be a Big Responsibility. She seems
to think that Big Responsibilities are bad,
but they're not. I'm in charge of cleaning
the whiteboard this week. Our teacher, Mr
Bacon, says it is a Big Responsibility. But
it's fun. Catie timed me this afternoon
and I cleaned it in forty-eight seconds. I
got marker ink on my sleeve but Mr Bacon
says it will wash out.

How can I persuade Mum to get a puppy?
What if my dream never comes true?
What if I spend my whole life puppy-less?

I will DIE of a broken heart!

I'm glad *Crookwatch* is starting. It's the
best programme on telly. It will help me
survive another long, puppy-less evening.

Later — in bed with ALL my cuddly toys to prevent puppy-less despair

Crookwatch was FAB. There was a story about a robbery in a supermarket. A man snatched money from a till. He got arrested, but NOT by a policeman! A customer stopped him as he tried to escape. They interviewed the shopper. He said:

"I saw this bloke running for the door and the checkout lady was shouting at him and pointing. So I grabbed his collar as he raced past and made a citizen's arrest."

HOW COOL IS THAT?

Who knew that *normal people* could make arrests! I thought I'd have to wait until I became a policewoman. But I don't. I could arrest someone right now! If there was a burglar climbing up our drainpipe RIGHT THIS MINUTE, I could wait for him to break in the window, then throw my duvet over him and tie him up with my bed sheet and ARREST him.

(BTW, I'm not *totally* sure I want to become a policewoman. I might decide to be an acrobat instead.)

OMG! If I became an acrobat, I could somersault after criminals as they made their escape. I could do a backflip and grab them

between my ankles and wrestle them to
the ground!

From now on, I'm keeping my eye on
everyone, in case they break the law. Next
time Jason Matlock drops a sweet wrapper
in the playground, I'm going to arrest him
for littering.

And if I get a puppy, I can train him
to be my police dog and he can *help* me
arrest people! ☺ ☺ ☺

I'd better turn my light out. Mr Bacon says
he has a special surprise for us at school
tomorrow. I can't wait to see what it is.

<u>Thursday morning – at my
desk in school, next to Catie</u>

A hamster. *rolls eyes* That was Mr Bacon's special surprise. He's our new class pet and we're meant to be excited. Sophie, Catie, Julie and Jenny are swapping notes about how cute the hamster is and doodling pictures of it in their jotters.

I'm glad they're happy because they're my best friends in the world. But hamsters aren't nearly as exciting as dogs. Why couldn't we have a class puppy? Mr Bacon could train it to take the register to the office. And to bark at the boys when they're being too noisy.

Imagine if every class had their own dog. Playtime would be awesome! There would be dogs running everywhere and we could throw sticks and balls for them. It would be the best game of fetch ever. I bet our class dog would love me most because he'd be able to *sense* how much I want a dog (dogs are very good at sensing things. On *Most Spooky* — my favourite ghost-hunting TV programme — family dogs are always *the first* to sense a ghostly presence) and he'd follow me around and I could train him to carry my lunchbox and to fetch Catie after she's been to band practice.

Hamsters are dull compared to dogs. You can't take them for walks. Or throw

sticks for them to fetch.
I bet hamsters don't even
come running when you
call their name. Ours is
called Squeak. Squeak?!?

I can think of a thousand better
names.

Butterball
Cupcake
The Fluff Monster
Little Wiggy Woogle
Cookie Nibblet
Mr Poopy

When Mr Bacon held up Squeak's cage and
told us he was going to be our class pet, I

put my hand up and suggested we call
him Eggs instead — so we could have
Mr Bacon and Eggs. But Mr Bacon just
said, "Thank you, Pippa. But Squeak already
has a name."

Then he told us we had to write a poem
about Squeak. We're meant to be writing
it now. Normally I love writing poems.
Rhyming makes me happy. I could totally
write a poem about dogs and how they're
better than frogs and never wear clogs
and you can take them for jogs.

But *nothing* rhymes with hamster.

Mr Bacon said that the person who
writes the best poem will be allowed to
take Squeak home for the weekend to look
after him. I don't even want to look after

a hamster. If Mum thinks I like hamsters, she might buy me one. And then I'll never get a puppy because there's no way Mum would agree to getting TWO pets.

Catie just showed me her hamster doodle. So I drew a puppy doodle next to it and wrote PUPPIES RULE underneath.

Then Jason Matlock started flicking pens at Darren. And Darren flicked them back, and then there was a pen-flicking fight across the desk. Mr Bacon stopped it, but if he hadn't, I was ready to make a citizen's arrest. I bet pen-flicking counts as Disturbing the Peace. (I learnt about Disturbing the Peace from *Crookwatch*. Crimes always have such good names, like Embezzling or Smuggling or Public Nuisance. I bet *most* boys count as Public Nuisances.)

I'd better work on my poem. Mr Bacon is looking at the clock and I need to hand something in before break time, even if it's not good enough to win the contest.

> I had a smelly hamster
> It peed upon the floor
> So I swapped it for a puppy
> Who I loved a whole lot more.

Catie's written four verses and Julie's poem fills a whole page. There's no way mine will win. Which is good.

My home is going to stay a pet-free zone until I get my puppy.

Thursday — at my desk, recovering from my packed lunch, which was cold spaghetti (Mum forgot to buy bread)

Actually the spaghetti wasn't that bad. But it had bits of broccoli in it and green food is just wrong.

ANYWAY.

Catie had the best idea while we were waiting in the classroom for the afternoon bell to ring. Mr Bacon hadn't arrived. Jason and David Jackson were

poking their fingers through the bars of Squeak's cage to see if he would bite them.

Freya was teasing Tom because his favourite football team lost their match last night. And Bossy Bethany was showing Mandy and Jane how to plait their hair *properly*. Apparently their plaits were twisted the wrong way and Bossy Bethany was *in heaven* because she loves telling people what to do. I was sitting on my desk with Catie while Jenny, Julie and Sophie flopped on their chairs beside us. I was telling them about my Dream Dog — it would have long fur and dangly ears and a waggy tail and big dark round eyes — and then Julie asked if I'd persuaded Mum yet.

I had to tell her "Not yet". So they started to invent ways to persuade her.

1. Go on hunger strike (impossible. I can't live without cookies ... or ice cream ... and I *definitely* can't live without chicken nuggets).

2. Get a T-shirt printed that says GET PIPPA A PUPPY! and wear it ALL the time.

3. Promise to wash up every night for a year.

4. Start an online petition. They all promised to sign it.

Then Catie told me how she persuaded her mum to get her a trampoline. (It's

AMAZING that Catie's mum agreed. She was convinced that Catie would fall off and break all her arms and legs if she tried trampolining. So I knew that if Catie's plan worked on her mum, it must be a BRILLIANT one.) My heart started leaping like an excited poodle when she said she had a plan. I leaned so far forward on my desk that I nearly fell off when she said, "You just have to google *How to get my mum to buy me a dog.*"

Isn't that genius?

The Internet has the answer to *everything.* It will definitely tell me how to persuade Mum to buy me a dog.

That's when Mr Bacon came in. He overheard us talking and said, "You are so lucky you have Google."

Then he told us something horrifying.

When he was at school, there was no Google.

IKR?

Mind. Blown.

Sophie asked him how he did his homework without Google and Mr Bacon explained that, if he didn't know the answer, he had to look it up in a book called an encyclopedia. I said an encyclopedia sounds like an insect with four hundred legs and long wiggly antennae. But he said it wasn't. It was a huge book with lots of information in it, like Wikipedia but with real pages, not Internet pages. Isn't it amazing that *encyclopedia* sounds nearly the same as *Wikipedia*? It's almost like the man who invented encyclopedias *knew* there was going to be a Wikipedia one day.

Mr Bacon is teaching us about the Roman Empire now. I wonder if he learnt about it from an encyclopedia? Was there really a book that contained all the facts about everything in the whole world? It must have been huge! I wonder where it was kept? Perhaps every town had a special building, as tall as a lighthouse. And the encyclopedia sat on the floor and reached right to the roof. And everyone in the town had to share it. Did people have to make an appointment to go and look something up? And did they need ladders to reach the bit of the book they wanted to look in? And what happened when someone discovered something new? Did they have to make a whole new book or did they just make an extra page and put it on top?

Later – after tea, at home

I googled! I found a great site with a long list called *How to Persuade Your Parents to Get You a Dog*. I'm going to try out one of the tips right now!

I've put my piggy bank on the kitchen table and stuck a label on it that says  Dog Fund. Mum looked at it suspiciously, then asked me how much was in it. When I counted out the money, I had £5.27. She said that wasn't enough to pay for a dog. But I told her we didn't have to *buy* a dog – we could get one from a dog shelter without paying anything. Then she told me that you do have to pay for dogs from shelters and asked who would pay for its food. I was ready with an answer straight away thanks to the website – I told her that I could earn money by washing cars for our neighbours and helping them weed their gardens.

She looked really impressed.

Then I raced upstairs to get the dirty washing basket. The website said that I had to show Mum that I am responsible enough to look after a dog by helping out around the house.

The washing basket is kinda big, so I rolled it downstairs. It left a trail of dirty washing along the hall, but before

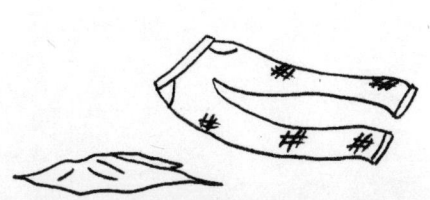
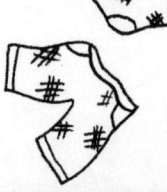

Mum could say anything, I scooped it up and started pushing it into the washing machine.

MUM: (*looking shocked*) What are you doing, Pippa?

ME: I'm helping with the housework.

MUM: (*still looking shocked*) Why?

That's when I knocked the washing powder box on to the floor.

I offered to sweep up the powder, but a lot of it was caught up in the clothes that were still hanging out of the front of the machine. While Mum went to fetch the dustpan and brush, I shoved everything in the machine, shut the door, scooped some of the spilled powder into the drawer at the top (I wasn't sure which section to fill, so I filled them all) and switched it on. I felt so proud when it started whooshing and humming, and when Mum came back with the dustpan, she looked surprised.

"Have you started it already?" she said.

I beamed at her. "Yes. In one hour and five minutes (I'd looked at the timer on the front) we'll have clean clothes."

I knew she must be impressed, especially when I grabbed the dustpan from her and swept up the spilled powder.

Then I offered to wash up, but Mum had already done it. So I had a bowl of cereal to make some mess. *Then* I washed up. Except, when I reached for the washing-up cloth, I knocked the instant coffee jar over and it fell into the washing-up bowl and turned the water brown.

Mum didn't get annoyed. She just looked puzzled.

"Why do you suddenly want to help with the housework, Pippa?" she asked. "Is it for a school project?"

"Kind of," I said. I didn't want to tell her about my puppy plan until I knew she was properly impressed by how helpful I can be.

She looked at the crumbs of washing powder on the floor and the dirty washing basket lying in the hall and the brown washing-up water and made a sort of hmpphing noise.

My tummy got butterfly-y. I could tell that I hadn't convinced Mum I was ready for a puppy yet. So I tried to think of another job that would *prove* I could clean up mess.

Hoovering!

I raced to the cupboard under the stairs and started pulling out the vacuum cleaner. But it sort of got tangled in the coats and scarves and shoes, and everything seemed to come out of the cupboard at the same time.

That's when the washing machine finished.

I left the Hoover-tangle and raced to get the washing out. As I hauled it into the washing basket, Mum came to watch. I was thinking that it was weird that all the clothes looked a bit different when I heard Mum gasp. She reached down, grabbed a shirt and held it up, looking horrified.

"It's pink!" she wailed. Then she grabbed a pair of knickers. "It's ALL pink!"

I stared at her, confused. "Isn't it meant to be?" Surely the clothes would turn white again when they dried? I blinked at the pink mass of clothes in the washing basket, thinking how happy Catie would

be if she knew clothes turn pink
in the wash because pink is her
favourite colour.

But Mum wasn't happy. She was
taking deep breaths like the ones
she uses when she's flustered
in traffic. A weird sense of
horror spread over me like I
was slowly being dipped in cold
water.

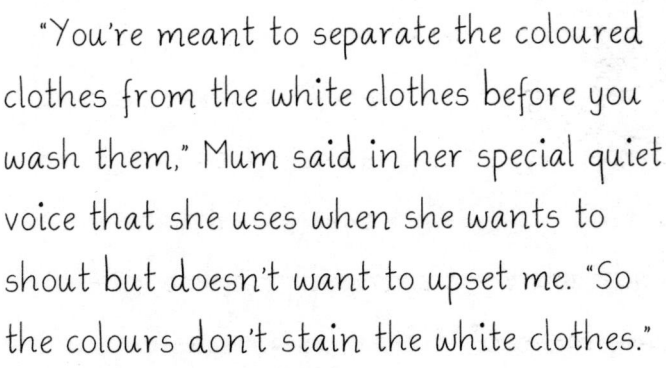

"You're meant to separate the coloured
clothes from the white clothes before you
wash them," Mum said in her special quiet
voice that she uses when she wants to
shout but doesn't want to upset me. "So
the colours don't stain the white clothes."

"Oh no!" My eyes started to get hot. I

could feel tears welling up. "I'm so sorry."
I was really *really* sorry. "I just wanted to
help."

"Oh, Pippa." Mum suddenly hugged me.
"I love that you want to help. But perhaps
you should start with smaller jobs."

"But then you won't see how responsible
I can be." I looked miserably at the pink
washing. Mum was never going to think I
could be responsible now.

"You don't need to be responsible for the
washing and hoovering."

"But I have to show you that if I have
a puppy, I'll be able to clean up after it!"

I blurted out my puppy plan and Mum
looked at me. "There's more to having a
puppy than cleaning up after it."

"I know!" I nodded eagerly. "I've researched all about having a dog. I need to take it for walks and train it to sit and feed it and give it lots of love. And I know I'll be great at all those things." I looked at Mum with my special pleading eyes. But she turned and started sorting through the basket of pink washing.

"Let's talk about it another time, Pippa, when I've sorted out this mess," she said. "You go and do your homework."

I know what "let's talk about it another time" means. It means NEVER.

It's hard to do homework while your heart

is breaking. But somehow I managed. I've done my maths and literacy and now I'm sitting in front of the computer. Mum's still trying to get the Hoover-tangle back into the cupboard under the stairs. I can hear her muttering something about "messier than a puppy". I think she means me.

There's nothing worse
In the universe
Than finding out that I will never
Have a dog that's smart or clever
Or a dog that's cute and fluffy
Or a dog that's fun and scruffy
I'll never have a dog, I think,
Because I turned the washing pink.

I wish I was better at helping with housework. Perhaps there's something else I can do to change Mum's mind.

Squeeeeee! I've just looked at the getting-a-dog website again and seen a NEW idea — "prove to your parents that you can take care of something — like a plant or a hamster."

AND I THOUGHT UP THE BEST PLAN EVER!

Mum knows that I've learnt all about looking after a dog, but if I bring Squeak home for the weekend and look after him really well, Mum will actually *see* that I'm ready to have a dog!

All I have to do is persuade Mr Bacon to

let me have Squeak and then be the best
hamster-looker-afterer in the whole world!

This is going to be so great!

Friday – lunchtime, at our favourite table near the window

I BEGGED Mr Bacon to let me rewrite my poem for the hamster-taking-home contest. I even had one ready:

Hamsters are great,
hamsters are fun,
They spin in their wheels
and sit in the sun.
They like to eat broccoli,
cabbage and carrots,
They're better than mice
and rabbits and parrots.

I read it to Sophie, Catie and the twins and they said it would DEFINITELY have won the contest. Then I told them about my plan to prove to Mum that I can look after a puppy by looking after Squeak for the weekend. Sophie said it was a great plan and Jenny and Julie said that looking after a hamster is probably harder than looking after a puppy because hamsters die more easily. (They've had four hamsters. All of them died. Not at the same time. That would have been a Hamster Disaster.)

Then I told them that I HAD to have Squeak for the weekend because I totally failed to show Mum I was responsible enough to have a puppy by helping with the housework. They were really kind when I told them about the pink washing. They know how it feels.

SOPHIE: I helped Dad paint the shed last summer, but I got distracted and accidentally painted over the windows and now it's so dark inside he needs a torch to find the lawnmower.

JULIE AND JENNY: We pegged out the washing in the garden last week, but we kept dropping it and it got all grassy.

CATIE: I once sprayed polish on the hall floor to make it nice and shiny. But I made it so slippery that when Dad got home from work, he skidded all the way into the kitchen.

Then Sophie offered me a crisp and Catie said I could have a bite of her sushi.
The twins even offered me some of their KitKat. The crisps and the KitKat cheered me up a bit (I told Catie that I didn't want her sushi in case it made my tuna fish sandwiches taste boring. Actually, I don't like sushi, but I didn't want to hurt Catie's feelings) but I know I shall never be truly happy again.

How can I be? My last chance of

convincing Mum that I'm ready to look after a dog has been STOLEN.

By Bossy Bethany.

Bethany won the contest! So she's going to take Squeak home for the weekend instead of me. She's showing off at her lunch table right now. Freya and Mandy Harrison are listening to her babble about how she's going to keep Squeak's cage in her bedroom to make sure he can't escape. (I would totally try to escape if I had to spend the weekend at Bethany's house.)

Poor Squeak won't be able to sleep BECAUSE OF HER SNORING. I bet when she brings Squeak back to school on Monday, he'll be so tired he sleeps all day. He'll probably be relieved to be back in the nice quiet classroom after listening to Bethany bossing her family about all weekend.

I can imagine her now.

BETHANY: Mum! You <u>must</u> clean out Squeak's cage. It smells of hamsters!

BETHANY: Dad! Go and buy Squeak some more food! *This* food is the wrong shape.

BETHANY: Everyone be quiet! I'm reading Squeak a bedtime story.

BETHANY: Quick! Clear a space on the table for Squeak's cage. I'm bringing him downstairs to watch *Animals Are Funny*.

I bet she even tries to boss Squeak about. She'll probably try to teach him to sit, or show him how to nibble sunflower seeds properly, or groom his fur the wrong way because Bossy Bethany always thinks she knows best.

I feel sorry for Squeak. I would HATE to spend the weekend with Bossy Bethany.

But there's nothing I can do to save him. Even though I begged my hardest, Mr Bacon wouldn't let me rewrite my poem. He said it wasn't fair on everyone else if I got two chances. If only he realized how important it was that I look after Squeak. I bet there's a puppy at the dog shelter RIGHT NOW, waiting to be loved. I KNOW I would love it so much it would be happy for ever. Instead, it's sitting sad and lonely without an owner. ☹

I must rescue it! I have to do something to show Mum that I'm ready for Puppy Responsibility!

Saturday morning – Dadville

I'm at Dad's flat. Mum dropped me off this morning. As soon as I got here, I asked Dad if I could have a puppy. But he said a flat isn't a good home for a dog. He said dogs need gardens. I promised to take it for a walk twice a day but he said what would it do in the flat while I was at Mum's. He works late and it's not fair leaving a puppy by itself for such a long time.

I wish puppies could play video games or read books or watch telly.

Then they would be happy left by
themselves all day because they wouldn't
get bored.

I wonder if there are day-care centres for
dogs like there are for little kids? Before
I was old enough to go to school, Mum
used to take me to a really nice nursery. I
stayed there while she was at work and it
was brilliant. There were SO MANY TOYS.
And other children to play with. A dog
nursery would be fab! There could be lots
of dog toys and comfy beds to sleep on
and a big garden for them to race around
and play with each other. If I don't become
a policewoman or an acrobat, I could run
a dog nursery. Imagine spending all day

playing with dogs? That would be the
BEST JOB EVER!

But first I need my own dog, so I can learn
how to look after it. If I can't have one in
Dad's flat, I'm going to HAVE to persuade
Mum.

Squeak is my only hope. Once she sees me taking care of him, she'll know I'm ready for a puppy. I hope Mr Bacon chooses me to take him home next weekend. I'm going to be extra good ALL WEEK so that he HAS to choose me.

I wonder what Bethany is doing with Squeak right now?

I can imagine her walking up and down her street with bows in her hair and Squeak in a handbag, showing him off to anyone she passes.

BETHANY: *(stopping a little old man)* Look, sir. This is *my* hamster, Squeak. Isn't he cute?

SQUEAK: *(poking his head out of the top of her bag)* Squeak!

BETHANY: I taught him to say hello to people.

SQUEAK: Squeak! (Help, help! Let me out of here!)

BETHANY: Later, I'm going to take him shopping and get a new handbag to match his fur.

SQUEAK: Squeak! (Please save me from this bossy girl!)

LITTLE OLD MAN: How lovely.

SQUEAK: *(sadly watching the little old man walk away)* Squeak! (Help! Rescue me from Bossy Bethany.)

And later she'll probably dress him up in old dolls' clothes. Poor

Squeak! I can picture him wearing a frilly pink dress and floppy hat while Bethany plays tea parties with him.

BETHANY: *(offering him a cup of pretend tea in a tiny cup)* Have a lovely cup of tea, Squeak.

SQUEAK: Squeak! (I don't want tea! I want hamster food!)

BETHANY: (handing him a plate of pretend biscuits) Would you like a chocolate biscuit?

SQUEAK: Squeak! (I don't want invisible biscuits! I want real biscuits!)

BETHANY: You're so cute in that dress! You're the cutest wittle hamster in the world! (tickles his tummy)

SQUEAK: Squeak! (I look stupid! Take this dumb hat off!)

If I have Squeak next weekend, I'm going to let him do *hamster* things, like run round in his wheel and kick sawdust around his cage and sit on his sleeping house and wash.

I COULD GET HIM A HAMSTER BALL!

He would totally love that. I can picture him now rolling it around the living room, his little hamstery face peeping though the plastic, all happy and excited.

He would have the best weekend ever!

Monday — at school. Thirty minutes before break

URGH!

Bethany brought Squeak back in his cage and she's ruined it! She's tied a BIG PINK BOW around the handle on top.

It looks STUPID.

And worse! Mr Bacon loves the bow and is going to leave it there ALL WEEK!

I bet Squeak is SO embarrassed. How would Bethany like it if I put a big pink bow on the roof of *her* house?

Actually, she'd probably like it. She's such a show-off, she'd probably stand outside telling everyone who passed that it was *her* house and the bow was *her* idea.

She's been talking about her "Weekend with Squeak" since she arrived at school this morning.

Things Bethany Has Said

1. Me and Squeak had tea together. I put his cage on the seat next to mine and we ate at exactly the same time. It was sooooooo cuuuuute!

2. Squeak knows what I'm thinking! When I was thinking about going

to watch TV, he started climbing up the side of his cage, as though he wanted to watch TV too. So I carried the cage downstairs and we watched *Go Dancing* together. It was sooooooo cuuuuute!

3. Squeak slept in my room. I could hear him scrabbling around in the middle of the night so I got up and read him stories until he fell asleep. It was sooooooo cuuuuute!

4. Squeak knows my voice. Whenever I call him, he runs to the side of his cage and looks at me. It's sooooooo cuuuuute!

I can't believe I ever thought hamsters were dull. I am going to HAVE to take him home this weekend, then I can take that stupid bow off and teach Squeak how to be a proper hamster again.

Perhaps the bow will disappear in the week. The janitor might think it's rubbish and throw it away. Or Mr Badger, the head, might say it's a fire hazard and take it off. Or Squeak might pull it through the bars of his cage and shred it. If I had laser eyes, I'd vaporize it right now.

Catie just poked me in the side. I was so busy writing in my diary I didn't hear Mr Bacon's Big Announcement.

He's going to be away for the rest of the week! He has to go to hospital for an operation but he'll be back next Monday. I was scared at first. Then Jason asked Mr Bacon if he had a contagious disease like the plague. And Tom asked if he was going to die.

But Mr Bacon just laughed and said, "No. You can't get rid of me that easily. It's just a routine procedure. I'll be fine by next week."

Catie squeezed my hand under the table. She must have been worried too. Mr Bacon is the best. I went to hospital to have my tonsils out when I was five. They gave me lots of ice cream but they wouldn't let me bring my tonsils home in a jar, which I thought was mean. They were *my* tonsils, after all. I hope Mr Bacon gets to bring something home in a jar and lots of ice cream too.

I wonder who our supply teacher will be. I hope they are nice. I need to be able to persuade them to let me take Squeak home. Last year we had a horrible supply teacher called Mrs Johnson. She was so strict, even Jason was scared of her. And the one before that had such a quiet voice, no one could hear her, and we just talked until our proper teacher came back.

I wonder where supply teachers come from. There's a big cupboard next to Mr Badger's office called the Supply Cupboard.

It's where Mr Bacon gets our notebooks and pencils. Perhaps there's a big cupboard somewhere far away with shelves full of supply teachers just sitting and waiting to be picked for a job.

Tuesday afternoon — after the most amazing morning at school ever!

Ms Beckwith is BRILLIANT! She's our supply teacher. She's not a Mrs or a Miss but a Ms. Ms Beckwith explained that it's pronounced "Mizz".

That is so cool. MizzMizzMizzMizz.

I've decided I'm going to be a Ms.

Ms Morgan.

Ms Pippa Morgan.

It sounds so grown up!

Ms Beckwith is the best supply teacher we've ever had. I'm glad they picked her out of the cupboard, although I bet all the other teachers are sad she's gone. They'll probably be bored without her, shut up in the dark, on their shelves.

Ms Beckwith is the Most Interesting Person in the World.

She wears a CAPE!

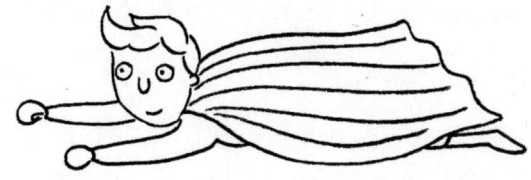

Not like Batman or Superman. Their capes look silly compared to Ms Beckwith's. Ms Beckwith's cape is long and swirly and dark green and velvety.

And she's not really a teacher. She's an ACTRESS!

She just does teaching when she is

"resting" between acting jobs.

She calls everyone "darling", which is so cool. Every time she calls Jason Matlock darling, he blushes as red as a tomato. He was quiet all this afternoon. I think he hopes that if he behaves, she won't notice him and call him darling.

When she came whisking into the classroom, her cape swirled a pile of books off the cupboard beside the door. Catie and me raced to pick them up and Ms Beckwith said "Thank you, darlings" in her loud treacly voice like she was the queen and we'd just saved one of her corgis from drowning.

Then she started the lesson. She threw
Mr Bacon's textbook about the Romans
in the bin and started telling us about
actors and actresses in Ancient Times
instead. She said their lives were far
more interesting than the dull lives of
"ordinary people" and that Mr Bacon could
teach us about "ordinary people" when he
got back.

I wish I'd been an actress in Ancient
Times. They got to play really good parts
in brilliant plays full of murders and
monsters. And they needed super-loud
voices to shout over the audience, who
used to heckle and chatter and throw
rotten tomatoes at the stage all the way

through the play.

I bet Ms Beckwith would have been a great ancient actress. Her voice booms around the classroom like thunder. It made the bow on top of Squeak's cage quiver. When Ms Beckwith saw the bow, she rolled her eyes dramatically and sighed. "Poor hamster," she said. "To live under a bow must be terrible!" And she took the bow off and twirled it in the air. "Bows belong on costumes, not hamsters." Then she leaned down to

Squeak and whispered loudly through the bars. "Now you are free to be a hamster, un-im-peeded by frip-purries."

I didn't know what she meant but I wrote it down straight away so I could look it up later.

Later – on the sofa

According to Google, "unimpeded by fripperies" means "unstopped by frilly things". Which I guess means Squeak doesn't need bows spoiling his fun.

Ms Beckwith is SO smart!

I want to be just like her.

I have decided to learn three new words every day.

My three words today are:

Mollycoddle
Hodgepodge
Eventide

I found them in an online dictionary. I

can't remember what they mean, but they sound really good!

As soon as I got home, I ran upstairs and found a towel so I could wear it as a cape. And I call Mum "darling" now.

ME: Darling, can we have pizza for tea?

MUM: *(looking at me as though I've gone insane)* Darling?

ME: I'm calling everyone darling now.

MUM: *(looking at my towel)* Why are you wearing a towel?

ME: It's not a towel, it's my cape, darling!

MUM: Are you playing superheroes again?

ME: Mollycoddle and hodgepodge! I'm far too old to play silly games like that. I'm going to be like Ms Beckwith and she wears a cape and calls everyone darling.

Before Mum could say anything else, I swept out of the kitchen and sank dramatically on to the sofa with my diary. Then I put the TV on, ready for *Crookwatch*. They use actors to re-enact the crimes. I wonder if Ms Beckwith has ever been on it?

Mum brought pizza in later. It was her special fried pizza, which is the best pizza in the world. And we watched *Crookwatch* together.

She didn't say anything else about my cape. But I could see her glancing at me out of the corner of her eye, as though she was checking I was OK.

I guess it's going to take her a while to get used to me being as fabulous as Ms Beckwith.

Crookwatch was amazing. There's been a crime in OUR TOWN!

IKR?

It was so weird to see streets I've walked down. ON TV! It felt like I was famous. The crime wasn't a scary one. Mum and me don't have to worry about burglars or escaped convicts. It was a woman who has been cheating old people out of their savings.

The cheating woman knocks on old people's doors and pretends she's doing a survey. Then she pretends her dog has just died and bursts into tears and sobs until they ask her in. Then, when they've made her a cup of tea and sat down with her in their living room, she starts telling them about a scheme that's about to make her rich. She promises they could be rich too if they give her lots of money. When they give her their money, she disappears and they never see her or their money again!

That is so AWFUL. Who could
steal money off an old person? I hope
the police track her down soon.
There was a photofit picture
of her, but photofit pictures
always look like cartoons. This
woman looks like a wicked
stepmother out of a Disney
film, but older and fatter.
I'm going to look out for
her, and if I see her,
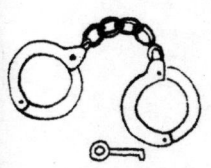
I'm going to make a citizen's
arrest.

<u>Wednesday – at school</u>

I think Jason has got used to being called "darling". He's stopped being quiet and he's back to his usual annoying self.

Ms Beckwith started the day by telling us what it's like to be an actor. She says it's a hard life, but a week marking homework is worth a minute on stage. She says when the lights hit you and the audience goes quiet, it's like entering another world.

Then Jason started asking stupid questions. He asked, "How come you're not famous?"

Ms Beckwith said, "I'm not famous <u>YET</u>." (She is SO smart!)

Then Jason asked, "Why haven't you ever been on telly?"

Ms Beckwith sniffed and said "telly" like she was talking about mouldy pizza. Then she said a TRUE actor learns her craft *in the theatre*. Then she said that she *had* been on telly once, because she needed some TV work for her CV. She'd been a pair of eyes peeping through a letter box on *Call the Doctor*.

I wonder if I saw that episode. Wouldn't it be cool if I'd seen Ms Beckwith even before she was our teacher? It's like we were DESTINED to meet.

Jason didn't seem impressed, but

Mandy Harrison pointed out that Jason had *never* been on TV — even as a pair of eyes. And Jason said he'd be on TV every week when he was a striker for Chelsea.

Ms Beckwith just gave him a huge smile and said, "Darling, your ambition is wonderful!"

Then she swirled her cloak over her shoulder (knocking the whiteboard markers off their shelf) and started teaching us maths.

It was the BEST MATHS LESSON ever!

Ms Beckwith believes in role play. She says: "You can only learn by being what you're learning about." So I was number three and Catie was number six and when we multiplied (we had to hold hands and dance in a circle saying the six times table) we made Freya, who was number eighteen.

Then we role-played long division, which was complicated because we all had to stand in the right place. One time, Darren stood in the wrong place and the answer was ten times bigger than it should have been.

The best bit was that each number had to have a different character. At the start of the lesson, Ms Beckwith told us what number we were. Then she asked us what our number would be like if it were a person. I decided that number three *looked* smiley (because it looks like two sideways smiles standing on top of each other) but it's secretly sad because it wishes it were an *even* number like two or four (even numbers are much better than odd numbers. They're WAY easier to add up and multiply).

After maths, we did literacy. Ms Beckwith said that the best way to learn literacy was to write "literature" (that's a clever word for books and plays). She told us each to write a play about Roman life. That's what we're doing now, and we're going to act out the best play before the bell goes.

Wednesday evening – after tea

What a brilliant day! We acted out MY play. It was about a Roman soldier who gets trapped under a cart and has to have his leg sawn off to get him out. I played the soldier because I'd written the play and Darren pretended to be a Roman doctor who had to saw off my leg so I could get free. While he was sawing with the cardboard saw Julie and Jenny had made, I shrieked so much that Mr Badger came in to see what the noise was.

He looked terrified when he saw the cart we'd built out of desks and me trapped underneath. He thought I was really stuck.

Especially when he saw the red felt-tip-pen marks on my leg, which Sophie had drawn on to look like blood. He turned pale and was about to call an ambulance when Ms Beckwith explained we were just acting. Mr Badger sat down on her desk and wiped his forehead with a hanky. Then he went to the staffroom for a cup of sweet tea.

After he'd gone, Ms Beckwith said I must

have "natural acting talent" because I'd convinced Mr Badger that the scene was real.

I nearly burst with pride!

When I went to Catie's house after school, we decided to practise our acting. Catie said I had to use my "natural acting talent" because it would be sad to waste it. First we had to have a snack, though. Catie's mum gave us organic hummus and carrot sticks. *shudders* Hummus tastes like cement. Poor Catie has to eat food like that all the time. Her mum makes *home-made* chicken nuggets. WITH SALAD! It must be awful.

ANYWAY...

While we were eating, Catie imagined me as an actress, starring in a big play in London. She said my name would be in big flashing lights over the doors and hundreds of people would queue up to see me.

I suppose if I *am* naturally talented, I must become an actress. It would be

unfair on my audience if I became a
policewoman. But perhaps I could still
be an acrobat as well as an actress. I'm
sure I could fit a few somersaults into
my plays.

Once we'd finally eaten enough carrot
and hummus to make Catie's mum happy,
we went up to Catie's big pink bedroom
and Catie pretended to be my mum and
I begged her for a puppy. It wasn't acting
really because I SOOOOOOO want a puppy.
Actually it was quite useful. I might use
some of the bits we rehearsed for real. We
even had a prop — Catie let me use her
cuddly hot-water bottle (which is
pink and fluffy and shaped like

a dog. She calls him Fwuffy) as my nearly
puppy.

CATIE (BEING MUM): No puppy for you,
Pippa! (she cruelly holds Fwuffy out of
reach)

ME (BEING ME): But Mother, darling! If
only you knew how I looooonggggg for a
puppy. (gazing longingly up at Fwuffy as he
dangles from Catie's hand)

CATIE (BEING MUM): It will mess up the
house.

ME (BEING ME): I will tidy up.

CATIE (BEING MUM): It will need feeding and walking.

ME (BEING ME): I can feed it and I love walking. I'll take it for five walks a day.

CATIE (BEING MUM): What about school?

ME (BEING ME): I can come home at lunchtime and take it out.

CATIE (BEING MUM): Won't you miss your friends?

ME (BEING ME): They can come with me. We can walk the puppy together.

CATIE (BEING MUM): What if it chews the furniture?

ME (BEING ME): I'll buy it a million chew toys!

CATIE (BEING MUM): *(giggling, which is what Ms Beckwith would call "being out of character")* What if it wees on the carpet?

ME (BEING ME): *My* puppy would never wee on the carpet. My puppy would be the best puppy in the world. It would love me so much that it wouldn't *want* to wee on the carpet.

CATIE (BEING MUM): *(looking stern)* No,

Pippa. You cannot have a puppy. That's my final word!

ME (BEING ME): *(throwing myself at her feet and hugging her ankles)* Please, Mother darling. Don't be cruel. If I don't have a puppy, my heart will break and burglars will stream through the windows and the house will burn down and there'll be no dog to warn us.

CATIE (BEING MUM): *(trying to look horrified but giggling even more)* Puppies only cause trouble.

ME (BEING ME): *(flailing dramatically on the carpet)* Oh, how can you be so heartless? My life is over. I have no reason to live!

As I spoke, Fwuffy's stopper must have come loose, because he started dribbling water over my feet.

CATIE: Look! He's actually weeing!

She was giggling uncontrollably as she twisted Fwuffy's stopper to stop the leak.

I sat up, trying to stay in character, which was hard when Fwuffy's "wee" was soaking through my socks. "How can I act if you keep giggling?" I asked her. Catie stopped for a moment, looked at me, then said dramatically, "To pee, or not to pee!" and exploded with laughter so hard that she sprayed me in giggle-spit. It was so funny, we collapsed into fits on the floor. It took us five minutes to recover.

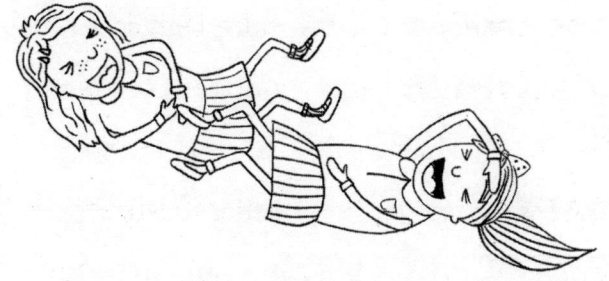

No wonder Ms Beckwith loves being an actor. It's fun!

Thursday — school

Best news EVER!

Ms Beckwith decided that we're not doing the poem competition this week to decide who takes Squeak home this weekend. I was a bit sad at first because my poem was so good this week. But then she announced that we are all going to have to perform a ~~sollillokwee~~ SOLILOQUY instead.

Jason thought a soliloquy was a dance and pulled a face and said dancing was for girls. Ms Beckwith said, "A soliloquy's not a dance, darling! It's a speech! You will each stand in front of the class this afternoon and recite a speech from your favourite film or fairy-tale character in your own words.

The best performer will be allowed to take Squeak home this weekend."

I am SO excited. It's the best idea ever!

Ms Beckwith wants us to choose our favourite film or book and give a speech about how it feels to be a character in it. Like pretending to be Cinderella and telling your story, or Mary Poppins, or the Incredible Hulk. She says that the person who puts the most feeling into their speech will win. How can anyone put more feeling into their speech than me? Winning this contest is the most important thing I will ever do. If I can't persuade Mum to get a puppy I will literally DIE. My life depends on me taking Squeak home on Friday!

Afternoon break

I was so nervous when Ms Beckwith announced that it was Soliloquy Time that I felt a bit sick. I'd been rehearsing in the playground all lunchtime with Catie, Sophie and the twins. They said I would win, but I wasn't sure.

My heart was hammering by the time Ms Beckwith started the contest.

She asked Jason to go first. He'd chosen James Bond. "Being James Bond is cool. I'm the world's best spy. I don't even know my boss's name. He's called M. I used to think it was short for Mike or Matt. But he's called M even when he's a woman, so I guess it's not. And there's a guy called Q who gives me cool gadgets. Playing with cool gadgets and travelling around the world on deadly missions is the best life ever. Plus I get to drive brilliant cars. And crash them. It's fun." Then he sat down. I felt a rush of relief. Jason hadn't put any feeling at all into his soliloquy. I was totally unmoved. I could tell Ms Beckwith felt exactly the same way as me because she just nodded and chose Freya to go next.

I knew Freya was going to put lots of feeling into her soliloquy, so I was nervous. Especially when she held her hands to her heart and looked at Ms Beckwith with large, round eyes. In a frightened voice, she said, "My stepmother is trying to kill me. Dad doesn't even care. She's been treating me like a servant since he remarried and he hasn't even noticed. Then she hired a huntsman to kill me. It's a good job I'm so pretty." Freya patted her hair proudly. "If I'd been ugly, he'd have killed me for sure. But because I'm so sweet and beautiful, he let me escape. Now I'm living with a load of dwarfs, which is quite nice, but I still have to do all the housework." She looked longingly into the distance, a dreamy look on her face. "Oh, I hope one day a prince will come and save me from all these chores and my wicked stepmother."

Putting her hand to her forehead, Freya dropped limply into her chair with a longing sigh.

Ms Beckwith applauded. "Well done, Snow White!" she hooted.

My heart nearly stopped. Ms Beckwith looked delighted. Had Freya won already? No! Ms Beckwith would be fair. I knew she would; she's a kindred spirit. So I decided to try doubly hard when it was my turn.

Ms Beckwith made me wait until last. By the time I stood in front of the class, there was only five minutes until break time. I knew I didn't have long. I was going to have to make my soliloquy as heartfelt as possible. So I clasped my

hands beneath my chin and began. "My
name is Perdita. I'm married to Pongo. I'm
a Dalmatian dog and I've just had
ninety-nine puppies.

Looking after that many puppies is the
best fun in the world. They are soft and
snuggly and we play all day and they love
me *so much.*" This is where I switched on
the super-emotion. I grabbed my throat
and looked horrified. "Actually, we *used
to* play all day, before Cruella de Vil *stole
them!*" I stared dramatically around the
class, letting them see how upset I was. I

actually felt truly upset. It's bad enough to yearn for *one* puppy, but to yearn for ninety-nine must be AWFUL. "Me and Pongo have looked everywhere for them, and all our dog friends are helping to search." I walked between the desks, my head held high like a proper actress, and stopped beside Squeak's cage. "Can you imagine how sad you'd be if you lost Squeak?" I gazed around the class, my heart nearly bursting with desperation. "Imagine losing ninety-nine Squeaks!" This was my chance to take Squeak home. The class was staring at me as though they couldn't wait to hear what I was going to say next. My heart swelled with hope. (Ms Beckwith is right: one moment on the

stage is worth a whole week's homework.)
So I went on.

"If Cruella goes ahead with her plan to make my dear, beloved puppies into fur coats, my heart will break into a thousand pieces. If only there was something that could comfort me in this time of grief. Perhaps if I had a hamster for the weekend, I'd feel better." I looked hopefully at Ms Beckwith, then, with a final sob, I said, "A hamster! A hamster! My kingdom for a hamster!"

Ms Beckwith had TEARS in her eyes! I could see them sparkling, and when she spoke, she sounded choked up. I knew I had moved her.

"Pippa," she gulped. "After a soliloquy like that, you deserve to take Squeak home tomorrow."

The twins started clapping and shouting, "Encore! Encore!" Catie and Sophie joined in, and before I knew it, the whole class were applauding me.

I bowed. A huge grin was spreading across my face. I'd done it! I'd got Squeak. I was so happy I could have exploded. I might have if the bell hadn't gone for break time.

Later – at home

The more you look at hamsters, the cuter they seem. Squeak seems nearly as cute as a puppy now (but not quite). I suddenly worried on the way home that Mum might have a secret hamster allergy or a fur-phobia. But she seemed really pleased when I told her and said we could keep him on the sunny table in the living room. I asked if he could sleep in my room at night and she thought that was a good idea, so long as he stayed in his cage.

She has no idea that this is what Ms Beckwith would call a "dress rehearsal". I'm practising for when I have a puppy. And when Mum sees how well I look after

Squeak and how HAPPY having a pet makes me, she will definitely get me a puppy.

I asked Mum if we could get him a hamster ball so he can roll around the living room. She grinned and said OK! We went straight to the pet shop and bought one. Squeeeee. I can't wait! I think Mum's excited too. I think she secretly likes the idea of a hamster rolling around the house.

Of course she does!

A HAMSTER ROLLING AROUND THE HOUSE IN A BALL!

What's not to like?

Friday — REALLY early

Mum's still snoring. I can hear her across the landing. It's three hours till school starts, but I am so excited about bringing Squeak home that I can't sleep any more.

Things I Will Do with Squeak

Feed him

Change his sawdust

Cuddle him

Feed him again

Put him in his hamster ball

Feed him

It's not a very long list. I'm sure I'll think of

more once he's home with me. (A *Things to Do with a Puppy* list would probably take up the rest of my diary.) I bet Squeak loves his ball, and I'll keep the cage with me all the time so he never gets lonely.

Mum said Catie, Sophie and the twins can come round after school to see Squeak. We can have a hamster party. Catie will have her trombone with her because it's orchestra day. She can play him a tune, and Julie and Jenny can do one of their songs where they sing in harmony. I can show Squeak how to do a handstand. Can hamsters do handstands? I guess it would be a paw-stand for Squeak.

This is going to be the best weekend ever!

Friday night – in the depths of despair

Today is the WORST DAY OF MY LIFE!

It's even worse than when I dyed my hair with scarlet paint to see what it would look like and covered the bathroom in big red spots.

AND the time I made a Lego cake and baked it in the oven.

I've done something SO terrible that everyone is going to HATE me.

I can hardly write it down, it's so bad.

Gulp.

Here goes:

Catie, Sophie and the twins came home with me. I carried Squeak's cage all the way. Mum was at home when we got there and she made us chocolate-spread sandwiches while I put Squeak's cage on the sunny table.

We decided to let him play in his ball straight away. Sophie said he probably needed some time out of his cage after being locked up there all week at school. So, very carefully, I opened the cage and lifted him out and put him in his ball. Then I put the ball on the floor and we watched him roll it around the carpet.

He looked so cute with his ginger fur and his little legs and his snuffly nose and his round black eyes, which are as shiny as shiny black buttons, and we kept giggling. Then Mum came in with the sandwiches and we sat on the sofa and ate them.

Then Sophie asked, "Where's Squeak?"

I wasn't worried at first. His ball had disappeared, but I guessed it must be under the sofa or the TV stand. So we started crawling around the carpet looking for Squeak.

Oh, this is so awful, I can hardly write it down.

Catie crawled behind the sofa and I heard her say, "Oh." There was something in her voice that made my heart drop into my tummy. I knew straight away that something was wrong, and I raced to look.

Catie was holding up Squeak's ball, and the door on the side was open, and...

I have to take deep breaths to calm myself now...

And...

SQUEAK WAS GONE!

He was missing. Completely disappeared.

We searched everywhere. Under all the furniture. In the living room and dining room and kitchen. We even looked upstairs in case he was a mountain-climbing hamster from Peru.

But we couldn't find him ANYWHERE. Catie and the others had to go home for tea eventually, but I kept looking until Mum said to sit down and have some dinner.

Where is he? *sob*

Mum says he must be *somewhere* in the house. Hamsters don't just disappear. She says we'll probably find him tomorrow.

I have to put my light out now because Mum just popped her head round the door and told me to snuggle down and go to sleep.

But I can't sleep knowing Squeak is lost somewhere in our house.

Midnight

A DREADFUL thought just made me sit up in bed like I'd been struck by lightning. What if Squeak ISN'T in the house? What if he found a mouse hole and squeezed outside?

If he's in the garden, a cat might get him. Or a dog, like Jason's. An owl might carry him off. I read somewhere that they eat mice and cough up their bones and fur in horrid pellets.

Poor Squeak! In a few days he might be nothing but a dried-up pellet lying at the bottom of an owl's nest.

And it's all my fault.

1 a.m.

What if Squeak crept up the Hoover pipe and got stuck in the Hoover bag? I saw Mum empty the Hoover once. It's full of dirt and dust. Squeak will choke if he's inside. Especially if he's asthmatic. Can hamsters get asthma? I should have asked Ms Beckwith if he had any medical conditions before I took him home.

<u>2 a.m.</u>

Perhaps he *has* got a medical condition.
Perhaps he had a weak heart and all the
running around in the ball made him
ill and he crawled out to die somewhere.
Apparently elephants all go to an elephant
graveyard to die. Perhaps hamsters have
hamster graveyards, full of little hamster
skeletons.

3 a.m.

Perhaps I knelt on him without noticing when I was crawling around on the floor. I might have squished him into the carpet.

4 a.m.

What if next door's cat sneaked in when
we got home from school?
It might have been waiting
behind the sofa for us to take
our eyes off Squeak. Then it
pounced and hooked him out
of his ball. AND ATE HIM.

Saturday morning

I got to sleep eventually, once the birds started singing and I could see daylight behind my curtains. The birds gave me hope. Lots of animals survive in the wild. Squeak must be OK. He HAS to be OK.

I'm going to find him today. I'll put piles of hamster food around the house and check them every five minutes to see if he's come to eat. He must be starving by now.

Later

Squeak didn't come to eat from any of
my food piles. Catie came round to help
me search for him. We tried looking in the
garden. We called his name under every
bush. I'm not letting Mum mow the lawn
until we've found him, even if it takes a
YEAR!

I've just had a great idea! Hamster
detectors! They'd be like metal detectors
except they'd detect hamsters instead. I'm
going to invent one when I grow up
so no child has to suffer like me ever
again. I can imagine me and Catie
scanning the lawn and the bushes with

our hamster detectors and then mine
starts to beep and we look down and
there he is! Squeak — the first-ever
hamster to be detected by a hamster
detector.

But we don't have hamster detectors, so we walked up and down the street. Sophie came to help, and so did the twins. We all called out "Squeak" as we went.

Mr Briggs from next door came out and asked us if we were pretending to be mice. I nearly cried when I told him, "I wish we were." I explained about my missing hamster and he promised to check his garden shed in case Squeak had hidden there.

Then Sophie had a good idea. She suggested we make some LOST posters — like people do with cats and dogs. So we drew some like this:

LOST HAMSTER

ORANGE + WHITE

ANSWERS TO THE NAME SQUEAK

REWARD: £5.27

Phone Pippa's mum on:

6749786

And Catie drew a picture of a hamster on each poster (she's best at drawing) and we stuck them on lamp posts along our road.

I wish I could offer a bigger reward than £5.27, but it's all the money I have in my Dog Fund. I don't mind giving my Dog Fund away. I don't need it any more. I'm not responsible enough to have a puppy. I can't even look after a HAMSTER! Sniff.

Sunday – The Worst Weekend of My Life

No one's phoned to say they've found Squeak.

I've searched the house twenty-seven times and I can't find him.

He must be an owl pellet by now.

And I've got to go to school tomorrow and tell everyone I lost Squeak.

My life could not be any worse.

I'll be known as the Pet Loser for ever.

And Mum will never let me have a puppy.

How could my brilliant plan have gone so horribly horribly wrong????

Monday morning

I'm still sweating with terror! I just woke up from an AWFUL nightmare. I dreamt I was watching *Crookwatch* with Mum and suddenly the man on the telly said, "You may find some of the following scenes disturbing."

In my dream, Mum wanted to turn the TV off, but I begged her to let us watch.

Crookwatch showed a re-enactment of what they called "the most awful crime ever", where an actress about my age knocked on an old lady's door. The girl was holding a clipboard and said she was doing a survey. When the old lady answered the door, the girl burst into tears and told the old lady her dog had died. The old lady felt sorry for her and invited her in and made her a cup of tea.

There was a cat asleep on the old lady's sofa. The girl said, "What a lovely cat," then she chatted to the old lady for a bit. And then she said, "I can look after your cat this weekend if you like."

And the old lady looked pleased and said, "Oh, would you? That would be so kind! I want to go to my nephew's fortieth birthday party and I was wondering who would look after Mr Squiggles."

Then the next shot was of the old lady staring sadly out of her window with a voice-over saying, "Mrs Turnball never saw Mr Squiggles again."

Then the announcer said that the girl had cheated three hundred and eighty-seven old people out of their beloved pets and that police were searching for her.

They showed a photofit picture that looked JUST LIKE ME.

In my dream, I leapt off the sofa and ran outside. All the lamp posts on our street had gigantic posters of me with WANTED: THE PET LOSER in big letters underneath.

I am officially the Worst Person in the World.

Everyone in the class will hate me. I'd hate me too if I didn't know how awful it feels to be the Pet Loser.

I'm going to beg Mum not to send me to school. I can't face it. Perhaps I can switch schools. I'll never see Catie or Sophie or Jenny and Julie again. But that's probably best. Why would they want to hang out with the Pet Loser?

Later

Mum made me go to school. She went with me to explain about Squeak. We walked across the playground with the empty cage. Everyone was there, waiting for the first bell. They looked at me and Mum and the empty cage, but I stared at my feet and pretended I was invisible so they couldn't ask me any questions.

I didn't want to go into the classroom so I stopped in the hallway and peered through the door. Mr Bacon was at his desk, marking books.

I was relieved to see him back at school. Ms Beckwith was ace but she might have made a huge drama out of a missing hamster. Mr Bacon can get really cross, but even if he gets cross, he doesn't wave his arms around or boom like Ms B.

He looked up when Mum steered me through the door. I could hardly look at him I was so MORTIFIED. I hung back while Mum quietly explained what had happened. I peeped from behind her, watching Mr Bacon's face now he was looking at Mum. She was explaining how I'd spent all weekend searching for Squeak, but Squeak was definitely lost. I was waiting for Mr Bacon to turn purple and steam to start coming out his ears.

But it didn't. Instead, he looked at me so sympathetically that I suddenly felt a bit better.

MR BACON: It was good of you to try so hard to find him, Pippa.

ME: I looked everywhere. Catie and Sophie helped. And the twins. We even put up posters all along our road.

MR BACON: It's sad Squeak has gone, but let's hope he's found a new home where he'll be just as happy as he was with us.

I hadn't thought of that. Perhaps Squeak

has discovered a community of escaped hamsters in one of the neighbours' gardens. Perhaps all escaped hamsters go there and they live happily in underground burrows, with little bowls made out of acorn cups and cosy beds made from socks stolen from washing lines. It might be the best place ever for hamsters.

They can hang out with their hamster friends and dig new tunnels and fetch seeds and grass from people's gardens for their dinner.

Suddenly I felt a whole lot better, especially when Mr Bacon said, "We can get a new class pet." I felt quite cheerful until I said goodbye to Mum. Then I remembered that the bell was about to go and the rest of the class would be back.

What would they say when they heard I'd lost Squeak?

Had they guessed from the empty cage? Had Catie told them yet? I started to panic.

Of course Catie hadn't told them. Nor had Sophie or Julie or Jenny.

When the bell went and they came into class, Bethany was the first to comment on the empty cage, which was sitting in its usual spot, except Squeak-less.

BETHANY: Did you forget to bring him back, Pippa?

DARREN: You're not allowed to keep him.

FREYA: (*looking worried*) Is Squeak OK?

That's when Mr Bacon asked everyone to sit at their desks and told them that Squeak had escaped and was missing.

I sat next to Catie feeling like a lump of stone. I could feel my face turning bright red but I couldn't move. I could feel everyone staring at me. No one said a word. Except Bethany, who gave a loud wail, then collapsed over her desk and sobbed.

I felt so bad.

Mr Bacon sighed and said that sad things happen sometimes and it's how we deal with them that's important.

Then Jason said, "Squeak's probably happier in the wild."

I stared at him in amazement. I thought Jason would be mean about it, but he just shrugged and went on. "I bet living in that cage wasn't much fun."

Bethany sobbed louder. "But he had a hamster wheel!"

Jason snorted. "Would you rather have a wheel to run around in or a whole garden to play in?"

Darren said he'd much rather have a garden, and Tom looked at Mr Bacon and said, "Does this mean we can have a new pet?"

Mandy Harrison suddenly looked excited. "Can we have a *lizard*?"

Everyone joined in then.

TOM: Or a snake.

CATIE: (*squeaking with fright*) No snakes!

SOPHIE: We could have a school cat. At

my last school there was a cat that used to walk in and out of the classrooms. He lived under the wooden fort on the playing field and the caretaker used to leave scraps out for him.

JENNY: (*looking excited*) A cat would be great! Mr Bacon, can we have a cat?

DARREN: I'm allergic to cats.

JASON: My cousin had a neighbour with a bald cat. We could get a bald cat. You wouldn't be allergic to that.

Then everyone started talking about bald cats and snakes and mice and tropical fish and a gazillion other possible pets for the class.

Except Bethany, who stared at me accusingly. "Squeak was my special friend," she hissed meanly.

Catie glared at her. "It wasn't Pippa's fault!"

"I didn't lose Squeak when he stayed with *me*," Bethany snapped back.

Jason butted in. "It's good that she lost him. Now we can get a *new* pet."

Then I wondered if someone lost me, would people get excited about getting a new Pippa?

TOM: Instead of Pippa, we could have Sally Murray from Mrs Webster's class. She's really funny.

JASON: We don't want another girl. We've just got rid of one. We should have Owen from Mr Atkins's class. He's a great goalie.

FREYA: There are too many boys in the class already. We need another Pippa, but one with curly hair. I knew a girl with curly hair once and she was really nice.

BETHANY: I think we should have someone more like me. Pippa was so bossy.

Then I started wondering what a replacement Pippa would be like. But then

I realized how sad Catie, Sophie, Jenny and Julie would be if I got lost. I imagined them sobbing at their desks like Bethany and decided to make sure I never got lost. That's when Jason suggested we get an elephant and Tom suggested a tiger.

Before everyone could start suggesting giraffes and chimpanzees, Mr Bacon told us to quietly make a list of our favourite animals while he did the register.

Tuesday – at school

Squeak is still missing and there's no new class pet yet. There's only an empty cage sitting beside the book corner. Mr Bacon said that we can think about what pet we want and vote on it on Friday.

I'm voting for another hamster. Even though I only knew Squeak for a few hours before I lost him, I now realize just how special hamsters are. But even if we do get another hamster, I'll NEVER get to take it home. Not now I'm a Pet Loser. ☹ I wish I could have a second chance to do it right. I need to prove to my classmates that I'm not a total failure. And I HAVE to show Mum that, even though I make mistakes, I can LEARN to be responsible.

I'm glad Mr Bacon is our teacher again. But I miss Ms Beckwith. We're doing history right now. Mr Bacon is making us write a page about the Romans in Britain. I'm going to write a play about Romans instead. I'm sure Mr Bacon won't mind. Ms Beckwith would have let us act it out.

I wonder what she's doing now. Is she teaching or acting? Perhaps she's working in a theatre. Or on a film shoot in an exotic location. Imagine if she remembers my performance as Perdita last week and begs to let me star in the film with her. Someone from the head's office would come

in with a note telling me I have to fly to
Spain at once to join Ms Beckwith on set.
There's probably a chair with my name on
it waiting for me under a palm tree, and
a make-up artist, and a costume designer,
all ready for me to arrive. That would be
fantastic!

Catie just whispered at me. She says I'm supposed to be writing about Romans, not film sets. *sigh*

I've just peeked at her workbook and she's written lots about Roman baths. Perhaps I should put a bath scene in my play. There can be a funny bit where Brutus slips on the soap. I wonder if there are other bits I've missed out. I'll write Sophie and the twins a note and ask what they're writing about...

SOPHIE, HAVE YOU WRITTEN ABOUT ROMAN BATHS? LOVE, PIPPA

NO. I'M WRITING ABOUT HOW ROMANS ATE DORMICE AND HONEY. LOVE, SOPHIE

I'M WRITING ABOUT ROMAN HOUSES.
LOVE, JENNY

I'M WRITING ABOUT ROMAN CLOTHES.
LOVE, JULIE

WOW! That's four more scenes for my play. Unless I write a long scene about Brutus going to the baths (and slipping on the soap) and then getting dressed in his special toga and then going home to his underfloor-heated house and having a meal of honey-roasted dormice.

This play will be so long, it'll be a MOVIE!

OH NO!

I've just had a terrible thought!

Did the Romans eat *hamsters* too? That would be awful! If Squeak had escaped two thousand years ago, he'd have been lunch.

Poor Squeak. I wonder where he is now. Is he really living happily with other lost hamsters in the wild? Or is he dead?

Tragic Ode to Squeak
By Pippa Morgan

Dear Squeak, please forgive me,
I didn't mean to be careless,
I hope you can live free,
All fluffy, and not hairless.
Did you make it to Cornwall,
or Wales, or to Devon?
Or are you just dead now and
living in heaven?
I can see you, an angel,
with wings like a dove,
A hamster with a halo,
looking down from above.

Tuesday – later

Catie, Sophie, Jenny and Julie came to my house after school and we held a memorial service for Squeak in my back garden. It was like the ones you see on TV for dead celebrities, except it wasn't in a cathedral and there weren't any famous people there. Instead it was just us, under the apple tree at the bottom of the garden.

We made a pile of stones on the grass and we each picked something from the garden to lay beside it as a sort of present for Squeak. I climbed the tree and picked the biggest apple I could find (they're not very big yet, but hopefully Squeak will still appreciate it).

Catie, Julie and Jenny picked bunches of grass with seeds on. Hamsters like seeds. Sophie had kept a few crisps from lunch and sprinkled them beside the stone pile. And Catie did the best thing. She'd brought her trombone with her, and she played a really slow, sad song while we all hung our heads and thought about Squeak and hoped that he was in a Better Place.

It was really moving. My eyes were all hot and prickly by the time Catie finished playing.

Mr Briggs from next door peeked over the fence to see what was happening. I was too choked up to speak, so Sophie explained. Mr Briggs offered to have another look in his shed, just in case Squeak was there now. But I shook my head. Squeak had been missing for so long, he had to be somewhere far away. So Mr Briggs found a toffee in the pocket of his gardening jacket and handed it over the fence so that Sophie could lay it beside the stones with our tributes. Then I picked a flower from Mum's flower border and put it on top.

It was probably the saddest thing I have
ever done.

Now I know how tragical it feels to lose
someone. I didn't realize how much I
loved Squeak until I put the flower on his
memorial.

I don't think I shall ever be happy again.

Friday morning – before school

I am sooooo tired. But tired in a good way. Since Squeak's memorial, I've been trying to be a better Pippa. A helpful and responsible Pippa. The sort of Pippa who doesn't lose hamsters and that Mums Are Proud Of.

On Wednesday, I mowed the lawn after school (I used the push-along mower while Mum used the electric one). Then I washed up after tea (without spilling any coffee into the sink).

On Thursday, I helped Mum make tea by chopping all the vegetables (very carefully) and then I brought down the dirty washing basket (without spilling any clothes) and sorted the washing into coloured piles and white piles. (The white pile wasn't very big. We have a lot of pink clothes now.)

I think Mum is pleased with me. She made me hot chocolate last night and said that we could do something special this weekend if I wanted.

But there's nothing special I want to do. Even after being so good, I still feel sad about Squeak.

Friday after school

OMG! OMG! OMG!

I can't believe it!

The BEST THING EVER!

I can hardly write I'm so excited. I think I might explode!

Mum came to pick me up from school today. And guess what she had with her?
  Trotting behind her on a lead...
  With floppy ears and big brown eyes and a wet, sniffy black nose...
  A PUPPY!

MUM BOUGHT ME A PUPPY!

I just stopped in the
playground and stared. I couldn't speak as
Mum reached the gate.

After my heart had leapt out through
the top of my head and flipped over like a
pancake before landing back in my chest, I
stopped breathing.

What if it was someone else's puppy?
Perhaps Mum was walking it for a
neighbour.

But then I saw Mum grinning a HUGE
GRIN. And I knew. It was OUR puppy. Her
eyes were all smiley like when she watches
me open my Christmas presents.

I ran over straight away and hugged

Mum and then the puppy and Mum told me to be gentle until he got used to me. So I let the puppy sniff my hands and I stroked him really softly.

Catie and Sophie came running across the playground. They were squeaking with excitement.

CATIE: Is it really yours?

SOPHIE: Is it a girl or a boy puppy?

CATIE: What's its name?

SOPHIE: How old is it?

CATIE: It's so cute!

SOPHIE: It's so small!

It was like they were saying all the thoughts that were rushing through my head OUT LOUD.

Mum answered all the questions: It's going to be Pippa's puppy. It's a boy. It's eight weeks old. Its name is Harry but we can change it if we want.

I definitely want to change it. Sherlock would be a much better name, or Wellington, or Frisbee. I've tried all three, but Harry still only answers to Harry.

Sophie and Catie crowded around him and petted him, swallowing back their squeaks when I told them not to frighten him.

But Harry was as excited as they were to say hello. He wanted to say hello to EVERYONE! His tail wagged harder and harder and he kept pulling on his lead, trying to sniff everyone in the playground.

I asked if I could hold the lead on the way home, but Mum said that Harry and me both needed puppy training before I could look after him properly. She's booked puppy-training lessons for us. I get to take him on Monday evening, and Harry can learn to *sit* and *walk* and *come* and do other puppy stuff, while I learn how to be the best puppy-owner ever!

On the walk home, Mum told me why she'd bought Harry. A lot of the reasons were from my list (writing lists is always helpful). Mum said that Harry would be good company for her, especially when I was staying with Dad. And also, after watching *Crookwatch*, she thought it would be a good idea to have a clever, loyal dog like Harry around the house to watch out for us. And she said that I'd been so good and responsible lately that she thought I was ready to look after a dog.

Isn't that great? I felt so proud. I kept bouncing around her saying "I love you!" and "I'm so happy" and "Thank you so much!"

And Mum just grinned and said she was glad I was happy again.

I'm going to go and see if Harry's awake.

He curled up in his basket when we got home (yes! We have a dog basket and dog bowls and chew toys and all the doggie accessories I ever dreamed of) and went to sleep. Mum says he's probably tired after all the excitement.

If he's not awake yet, I'll just sit quietly beside his basket and stroke his ears. They are so soft. Even softer than Squeak's.

Harry is officially the best dog in the world!

Later – camping in the kitchen

Harry did something so amazing after tea that I think he should win a special award.

(I'm writing this with a torch so I don't wake Harry up. He's asleep in his basket beside me. Mum said he had to sleep in the kitchen but I said he'd be lonely. So I asked if I could sleep in the kitchen too and Mum said OK. So I brought down my camping mattress and my duvet and all the spare pillows I could find and I made a special tent out of a sheet and the kitchen chairs and snuggled down beside him. He wagged his tail the whole time even though he was sleepy. And once I'd finished making my tent-bed, I stroked his ears till he fell asleep. I LOVE HIM SO MUCH!)

ANYWAY.

He did this amazing thing!

Harry's Amazing Thing

We were watching *Crookwatch*. (They caught the cheating woman, BTW. A clever granny recognized her from the photofit picture and invited her in and called the police while she was making her a cup of tea.) Harry kept sniffing the side of the sofa. Mum told him to stop, but he kept sniffing and sniffing and getting more and more excited, like there was a dog biscuit inside. So I crouched down on the carpet beside him and started sniffing like I was a puppy too. That's when I heard scrabbling inside the sofa.

I screamed at first, in case it was a giant puppy-and-Pippa-eating spider.

So Mum sent me and Harry to hide in
the kitchen with the door closed while
she tipped the sofa over and had a look
inside.

The next moment, she
flung open the kitchen door.
I couldn't believe my eyes. She
was holding Squeak in her
hands!

He's been living inside the
sofa. Mum found a nest he'd
made out of shredded-up newspaper. Isn't
he clever? And isn't Harry super-clever for
finding him?

We put Squeak inside a shoebox
with holes in the top and some of
the straw and hamster food we had

left over from the weekend. I can take
him back to school tomorrow. Everyone
is going to be amazed. Especially when
I tell them it was HARRY who found
him.

The class will have their pet back.
And I have my OWN pet at last.
Harry is a hero. He's like
a police dog! Oh wow, that's
brilliant! He can be my loyal
sidekick and help me when I
make citizen's arrests. ☺
I'M SO HAPPY!!!!

I can't wait till
Friday and our
first puppy-
training lesson.

I'm going to learn *everything* so I can look after Harry better than anyone else in the world.

I'm not the Pet Loser any more! I'm the Puppy Owner!
  SQUEEEEEEEEEEE!!!!!!! ☺ ☺ ☺ ☺

THE PET OWNER

<u>SEVEN REASONS WHY</u>
<u>PIPPA LOVES HARRY</u>

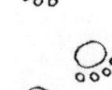

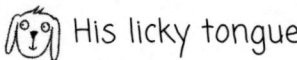 His licky tongue

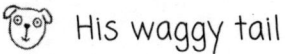 His waggy tail

 His furry face

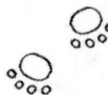

 His soft ears

 His wet nose

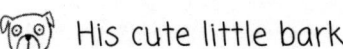 His cute little bark

 His perfect paws

A POEM FOR HARRY

Harry you're the greatest dog,

Waaay better than a slimy frog.

I love the way you lick my face

And helped me solve the Lost Hamster case.

Puppy darling je t'adore,

Even when you wee on the floor!

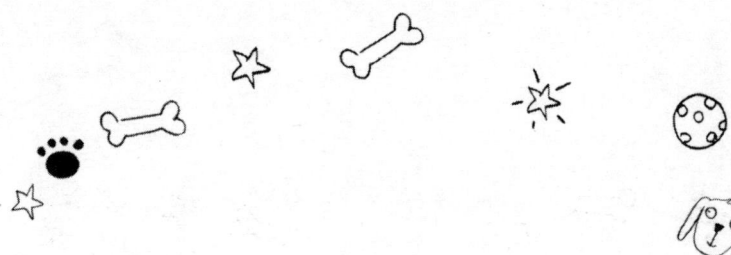

OTHER POSSIBLE NAMES FOR HARRY

~~Sherlock~~

~~Wellington~~

~~Frisbee~~

Chicken Nugget

Puppy Morgan

Snuggly Bear

Sniffany J (after my hero Tiffany J)

Hairy

Darling Dog

Hamsters vs. Dogs

	Hamsters	Dogs
Furriness	☺☺	☺☺☺
Cuteness	☺	☺☺☺☺
Waggiest Tail	☹☹☹	☺☺☺☺
Cuddleability	☹☹	☺☺☺
Messiness	☺☺	☹☹
Stick catching	☹☹☹☹	☺☺☺☺
Total:	☹ = 9 ☺ = 5	☹ = 2 ☺ = 18

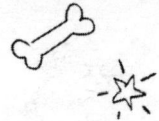 

PIPPA'S TIPS FOR BEING A PET OWNER

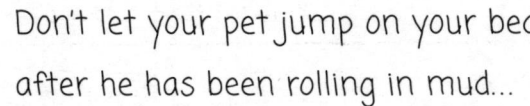

Don't let your pet jump on your bed
after he has been rolling in mud...

Don't accidentally let your pet eat
Mum's Fried Pizza...

Do give your pet lots of hugs and kisses
(unless it's a jaw-chomping crocodile).

Do take your pet for lots of walks
(unless it's a super-slow, slimy snail).

Do teach your pet lots of cool tricks. (I'm
teaching Harry to sit, fetch and hunt
down criminals!)